HUMAN BODY
LAB

THE ULTIMATE HUMAN BODY PACK

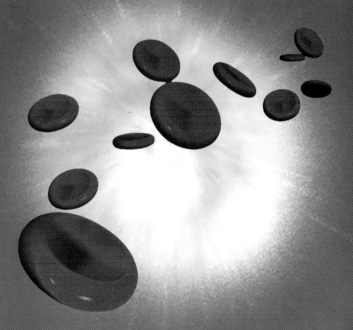

HUMAN BODY LAB is a fascinating guide to the human body. Your body is an amazing structure, and you can learn all about how it functions by performing the experiments inside this manual. Discover how the different systems in the body work together and use the equipment in the kit to help you perform the experiments successfully.

MANUAL

LABORATORY

C O N

All of us share one thing in common—a body! Over the centuries, scientists and doctors have made new discoveries about how we think, feel, see, hear, taste, and smell; how muscles and bones support and move our bodies; and how the blood carries vital oxygen and digested food through the body to supply the needs of trillions of cells. Now you, too, have the chance to be a body scientist.

Investigate the human body and discover more about how it functions. Read on and try out the experiments in *Human Body Lab*.

T E N T S

LABORATORY

1

Your body is a remarkable structure. Its many components work together to produce the walking, talking, thinking being that is you. Throughout this book, you will find out how this happens.

BUILDING BLOCKS

Every human body is made up of trillions of cells, each one a microscopic living unit. There are about 200 different types of cells, such as muscle cells, bone cells, and blood cells, in your body. Groups of cells of the same or similar types form a tissue, like muscle tissue, in order to carry out a particular job. Two or more tissues are linked together to form organs such as the stomach, which have one or more specific roles. A group of linked organs forms a system, such as the digestive system, which has one major job to do. Systems work with each other to form a complete body.

Molecules make up cells.

Similar cells from the stomach

Tissues from the stomach wall

The stomach forms part of the digestive system, one of the twelve systems that make up the body.

Different tissues make up this organ, the stomach.

4

As you read the lab manual, you will encounter and investigate many of the body's systems. The nervous system controls your body and lets you see, hear, feel, and think.

The integumentary (covering) system consists of the skin, hair, and nails, and covers and protects your body. The bones of your skeletal system support your body and, together with the muscular system, enable it to move. The circulatory system moves blood around your body, carrying supplies to your cells. The respiratory system gets life-giving oxygen into your body, while the digestive system brings in vital food supplies.

DID YOU KNOW?

Some body cells live for just a few days before being replaced, while others last for many years. For example, cells lining the small intestine (where food is digested) survive for about three days before being carried away by passing food. The doughnut-shaped cells that make up red blood cells live for about 120 days before they are replaced. Many neurons (nerve cells) last a lifetime, but each day the brain loses about 1,000 neurons, which are not replaced.

1

COMPLETING THE POSTER

Accompanying this book is a fascinating, life-size poster of the body. There is also a set of stickers of certain body organs. In this activity, your goal is to locate where each organ is found in the body and put the sticker in the correct place.

1 Look at the first sticker. Match it to the clue on the poster that describes that organ.

2 Once you have found the correct match, put the sticker on the poster.

WHAT HAPPENS?

Once in place, the stickers show the locations of the body's most important organs. You now have a life-size body guide that you can refer to as you carry out the experiments in the book.

LABORATORY 2

Every aspect of your behavior is controlled by your brain and nervous system, whether it's your thoughts, ideas, memories, senses, or movements. Here you can see your brain and nervous system at work.

BRAIN POWER

Your nervous system contains billions of neurons, or nerve cells, that carry electrical signals, called *impulses*, at high speed. At its center is your brain, which is linked to the rest of your body by the spinal cord and nerves. The nerves carry information to the brain from sensors, such as eyes and ears, and relay instructions from the brain to the muscles, telling them what to do.

Brain

Spinal cord

Nerve

REACTION TIMES

You are constantly reacting rapidly to changes in the world around you. How quickly can you react?

1 Ask your assistant to hold the ruler vertically by its tip.

2 Place your open thumb and forefinger just below the bottom of the ruler, about half an inch apart.

3 Tell your assistant to let go of the ruler without any warning. As soon as you see it drop, grab it between your thumb and forefinger. Make a note of the measurement on the ruler where you grabbed it.

4 Repeat this several times.

WHAT HAPPENS?
The closer your gripping finger and thumb are to the bottom of the ruler, the faster your reaction time. You should find that your reaction time improves with practice.

TRY THIS
Put on a blindfold and repeat the experiment. This time your assistant should say "drop" when he releases the ruler. You should find that your reaction time is slower, as it takes longer for your brain to process the sound of your assistant's voice than it does to process the sight of the ruler dropping.

YOU WILL NEED: **1**
• ruler
• blindfold
• assistant

YOU WILL NEED: **2**
• assistant

YOU WILL NEED: **3**
• 9 cocktail
  sticks

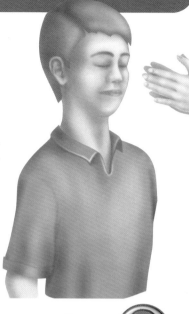

2
REFLEX ACTION

Reflex actions—such as pulling your hand away from a hot object—happen quickly and automatically, without thinking. Find out more with this experiment.

1 Ask your assistant to stand up, facing forward. Stand next to him.

2 Without warning, clap your hands just in front of his face. What happens to his eyes?

WHAT HAPPENS?
Your assistant will blink immediately. This blinking reflex protects the eyes from possible damage.

DID YOU KNOW?
It takes just one-thirtieth of a second for you to pull your hand away from a hot object.

3
PROBLEM SOLVING

You use your brain every day to solve problems. Test that brainpower with this puzzle.

1 Arrange nine cocktail sticks in the pattern of the triangles shown above.

2 Move just three cocktail sticks to make five triangles.

WHAT HAPPENS?
The solution is somewhere else in this book. Use your brainpower to find it!

DID YOU KNOW?
There are over 100 billion (100,000,000,000) neurons in the human brain. Each brain neuron can have connections with thousands of other neurons, producing an incredibly complex communication and processing network.

BEHAVIOR

GOOD

Vision is the most important of the senses. When sensors in your eyes are hit by light, they send messages to your brain, which enable it to form pictures of the outside world.

LIGHT DETECTORS

From the outside, only the front part of an eyeball (formed by the cornea, iris, and pupil) is visible. The rest of the eyeball is protected within a bony socket in the skull. Its inner lining, the retina, is filled with light sensors called *rods* and *cones*. These send nerve impulses along the optic nerve to the brain.

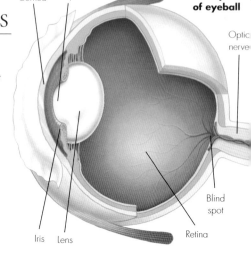

Cornea   Pupil

Cutaway view of eyeball

Optic nerve

Blind spot

Iris   Lens

Retina

1
PUPIL POWER

The pupil is a hole that allows light into the interior of your eyeball. Its size is controlled by the colored iris that surrounds it. Investigate how it changes size.

1 Find somewhere where the light is not bright. Using the mirror, look carefully at one of your eyes. Note the size of the pupil.

2 Ask your assistant to shine a flashlight at your eye. What happens to your pupil?

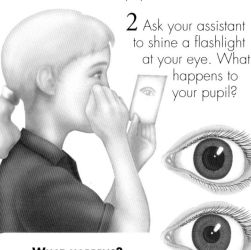

WHAT HAPPENS?
In dim light, your pupils are wide. This lets in enough light for sensors to fire off signals to your brain. In bright light, your pupils shrink. This reduces the amount of the light entering your eye, so your retina is not damaged.

2
VANISHING POINT

There is one part of the retina that cannot detect light. This experiment will reveal all!

+   •

1 Hold this page in front of you and look at the "cross and dot" picture above, about 18 inches away from your eyes.

2 Close your left eye and look at the cross with your right eye.

3 Slowly bring the book toward your face. What do you notice?

WHAT HAPPENS?
At a certain point, the dot disappears. This is because the light from it lands on a part of the retina called the "blind spot," where the optic nerve leaves the eye and where there are no light sensors. Your brain normally fills in this gap so that you do not notice it.

YOU WILL NEED: 1
- mirror
- flashlight
- assistant

YOU WILL NEED: 2
- blind spot test (on previous page)

YOU WILL NEED: 3
- optical illusion cards
- ruler

YOU WILL NEED: 4
- colored pencil
- assistant

3
EYE TRICKS

Can you believe everything you see? Try the optical illusions on this page and on the cards in the kit to see if you can!

WHAT HAPPENS?
Your brain sorts out the signals from the eyes so that you can actually see something. To do this, it uses various clues to make sense of an image. But in the case of these visual tricks, the clues are confusing.

1 Phantom triangle: Look at this picture and you will probably see two triangles. Now look more closely and you will realize that there is only one triangle. Your brain assumes, wrongly, that the circles with a segment cut out are each the point of a triangle. It fills in the missing lines, so you think you are seeing another triangle.

2 How long? Which of these two lines is longer? The one on the right? In fact, they are both the same length. Check this with a ruler. It's the slanted lines at the ends that make the line appear shorter (left) or longer (right) than it really is.

4
IN COLOR

Can you see an object in as much detail from the corner of your eye than you could if it were right in front of you? Find out here.

1 Ask your assistant to sit down and look straight ahead.

2 Pick up a colored pencil (unseen by your assistant) and bring it slowly around the back of his head toward the front.

3 Ask your assistant (a) when he can identify the object and (b) when he can tell you its color.

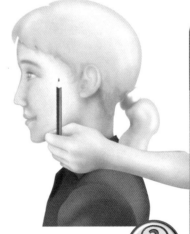

WHAT HAPPENS?
Your assistant will be able to identify only what the object is, and then tell you its color as the pencil moves closer to the front. At the side of the head, light from the pencil falls on rods that only see in black and white. Further around, light falls on cones that see in color and provide the brain with a more detailed view of objects.

From the soft buzzing of an insect to the roar of a jet, your ears detect a wide variety of sounds. Now learn how they also play a part in keeping you balanced and upright.

ALL EARS

Sound waves travel though the air from a vibrating source, such as a plucked violin string, into the ear. Sound waves make the eardrum vibrate, sending the vibrations along a chain of bones to the cochlea. This fires off nerve messages to the brain, which interprets them as sounds you can hear.

Semicircular canal (balance sensors)

Ear canal

Eardrum

Chain of small bones (ossicles)

Cochlea

Cross section of the ear

1

WHICH DIRECTION?

How do you know where a sound is coming from? Try this experiment to find out more.

1 Ask an assistant to volunteer to wear the blindfold.

2 Arrange yourself and your remaining assistants in a circle, with the blindfolded person standing in the center. One person should sit directly in front and one directly behind him.

3 Ask people to clap their hands at random. After each clap, ask the blindfolded person to point to the sound's source. How accurate is he at identifying the source?

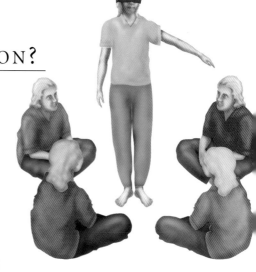

WHAT HAPPENS?

Sounds usually reach one ear a split second before the other. Your brain uses this tiny time difference to work out the sound's direction. Using your eyes provides extra information to the brain. Even blindfolded, your assistant should be able to point toward the source of a sound. He will, however, find it difficult to distinguish sounds coming from directly in front or behind because those sounds arrive at both ears at the same time.

② SOUNDS DIFFERENT

Does your voice sound the same to you as it does to other people? Try this experiment to find out.

1 Use a tape recorder to record your voice.

2 Play your voice recording back. Do you notice anything different?

③ OFF BALANCE

How do you manage to stay upright when standing or walking? Find out here, noting with each step how easy it is to stay upright.

1 Take off your shoes and socks, put on the blindfold, and stand on the cushion, with your arms out to the sides.

2 Now stand on one leg on the cushion, with your arms out.

3 Repeat Step 2 with your arms by your side.

WHAT HAPPENS?
Your recorded voice sounds different than your spoken one. Sound waves from the tape recorder travel directly to your ears through the air. But during normal speech, sound vibrations also vibrate through the bones of your skull, giving your voice a different quality.

WHAT HAPPENS?
Balancing gets progressively more difficult with each step. Your brain loses the information it needs from feet sensors and the eyes to help you balance. By the end of the experiment you are depending only on sensors in your ears (semicircular canals), making you wobble quite a bit.

RIGHT

SOUNDS

Imagine if you couldn't enjoy the aromas and flavors of your favorite meal. Fortunately, your senses of smell and taste allow you to do just that. Investigate those senses in action.

LINKED SENSES

Smell and taste are closely linked senses. Both senses detect tiny chemical particles called *molecules*. Smell detectors are found inside the nose and they detect odor molecules in the air you breathe. Taste receptors in the taste buds on your tongue detect taste molecules in food and drink.

Smell detectors

Nasal cavity

Mouth

Tongue

Cross section of the head

2
TELL BY SMELL

How good do you think your sense of smell is? Could you pick out different substances by smell alone, without being able to see them?

1
BUMPY TONGUE

Is the surface of the tongue flat or bumpy? Have a look and find out.

1 Ask your assistant to poke out his tongue.

2 Use the magnifying glass to look at the surface of the tongue. What do you see?

1 Blindfold your assistant.

2 Ask an adult to cut the various smelly substances into chunks. Put each substance onto its own plate and cover it with a glass to trap its smell.

3 Take the first plate and lift the glass. Can your assistant identify the substance by smell?

4 Repeat Step 3 with the other substances.

WHAT HAPPENS?
The surface of the tongue is rough and covered by tiny projections called papillae. *Round papillae contain the taste buds, while spiky ones help your tongue grip food as you chew it.*

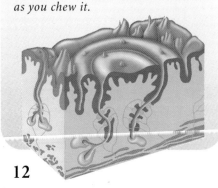

WHAT HAPPENS?
Your assistant will probably find some things, especially the foods, easier to identify by smell alone. Other substances may be more difficult, as sight helps you recognize the smell of certain substances.

YOU WILL NEED: **1**
- magnifying glass
- assistant

YOU WILL NEED: **2**
- blindfold
- assistant
- 6 common food and nonfood substances with distinctive odors, e.g., soap, onion, candle wax, lemon, cheese
- kitchen knife
- 6 small plates and glasses
- adult supervision

YOU WILL NEED: **3**
- blindfold
- noseclip
- assistant
- 6 foods with distinctive flavors, e.g., chocolate, pineapple, cheese, pear, onion, lemon
- kitchen knife
- fork
- 6 small plates
- notepad and pen
- glass of water
- adult supervision

WARNING! CHECK WITH YOUR ASSISTANT TO SEE IF THEY HAVE ANY FOOD ALLERGIES BEFORE CARRYING OUT THIS EXPERIMENT.

3
LOSING FLAVOR

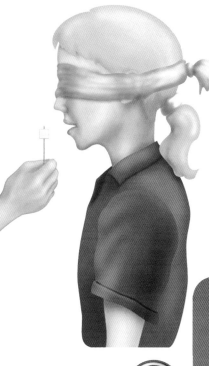

Working together, your senses of smell and taste allow you to detect flavors. How easy is it to identify flavors using just your sense of taste?

1 Blindfold your assistant and put a noseclip on his nose.

2 Ask an adult to cut the food into equal-size pieces and put each type on separate plates.

3 Spear the first food item on the fork and gently rub the item on your assistant's tongue. Can he identify the food?

4 Tell your assistant to rinse his mouth with water, then try the other foods in turn.

WHAT HAPPENS?
Your assistant should find it difficult to identify the foods. Both senses—smell and taste—are needed to pick out flavors. You have removed their sense of smell, which is 20,000 times more sensitive than the sense of taste.

TRY THIS
Remove the noseclip from your assistant's nose and repeat the experiment. With the added benefit of smell, he should find it easier to identify some of the foods.

DID YOU KNOW?
Your senses of smell and taste also provide warning signals. A smell of burning may signify danger, while bad-tasting food may be poisonous and should be spat out.

AROMAS AND

FLAVORS

Skin forms a flexible, waterproof barrier that protects the delicate inner parts of your body from the harsh conditions outside. Take a closer look at your skin to see how it works.

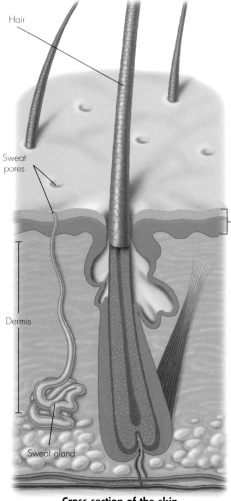

Hair

Sweat pores

Dermis

Epidermis

Sweat gland

Cross section of the skin

TWO LAYERS

Your skin is made of two layers. The tough, waterproof epidermis keeps germs out and protects you from the harmful rays of the sun. The thicker dermis contains blood vessels, hair roots, and sweat glands, which release cooling sweat onto the skin's surface.

BUMPY SURFACE

How well do you know your skin? It's time to find out!

1 Using a magnifying glass, look carefully at the skin on the back of your hand. Is it smooth or wrinkled? How hairy is it?

2 Now look at other parts of your skin. Do they all look the same?

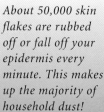

DID YOU KNOW?
About 50,000 skin flakes are rubbed off or fall off your epidermis every minute. This makes up the majority of household dust!

WHAT HAPPENS?
Your skin's surface is crisscrossed by creases and grooves. Some parts are hairier and some are smoother. Your palms and the undersides of your fingers have no hair, but have ridges that help you grip objects.

YOU WILL NEED:
• magnifying glass **1**

YOU WILL NEED:
• small plastic bag
• rubber band
• dropper/pipette **2**

YOU WILL NEED: **3**
• 2 adult assistants, one older than the other
• stopwatch or a watch that shows seconds

2 COOLING SWEAT

Sweating helps cool you down. But even when it's not very hot or when you are sitting still, your body sweats.

1 Put the plastic bag over your hand. Seal the bag—not too tightly—using a rubber band.

2 Leave the bag in place for 15 minutes. What do you see?

WHAT HAPPENS?

Tiny drops of moisture appear on the inside of the bag. When sweat is released onto the surface of your skin, it draws heat from your body and evaporates, forming water vapor. This condenses (forms droplets) on the plastic bag. Sweating helps your body temperature stay constant at 98.6°F.

TRY THIS
Use the dropper to drop a few drops of perfume on your skin. As the perfume evaporates it takes heat from your body. You should feel your skin cooling.

3 SUPPLE SKIN

Discover how supple your skin is, then compare it to the skin of older people.

1 Gently pinch a fold of skin on the back of your hand.

2 Hold the skin away from your hand for 30 seconds, then let go. Time how long it takes the skin to go flat again.

3 Repeat the experiment with two adults of different ages.

WHAT HAPPENS?
Your skin bounces back faster than that of the adults. The dermis contains elastic fibers that allow the skin to stretch and then return to its normal shape. As people get older, these fibers shrink and become less flexible. That's why the skin of older people is less supple.

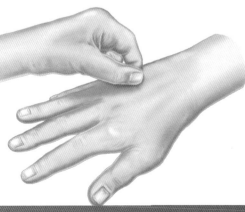

DEEP SKIN

LABORATORY
7

Millions of tiny touch sensors are scattered throughout the skin. They send messages to the brain, which tells you what you are feeling. These experiments show your skin sensors at work.

SKIN SENSATIONS

Your skin contains a range of different sensors. Near the surface are free nerve endings that detect heat, cold, and pain, in addition to sensors for light touch and pressure. Deeper sensors detect heavy pressure and vibrations. Messages from these sensors allow your brain to produce a "touch picture" of your surroundings.

Cross section of the skin showing sensors

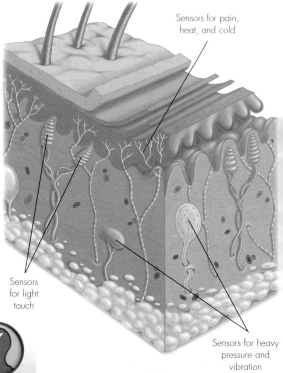

Sensors for pain, heat, and cold

Sensors for light touch

Sensors for heavy pressure and vibration

DID YOU KNOW?

Many blind people are able to read using their fingertips. They use the Braille system, in which letters are replaced by raised dots on a page. The person reads by feeling these raised dots.

1
DIFFERENT TEXTURES

You feel different touch sensations according to which sensors in your skin are stimulated. Use an assistant to test this.

1 Blindfold your assistant.

2 Ask your assistant to feel each part of the touch strip and describe what he feels using just one word.

WHAT HAPPENS?

Your assistant should use words such as "soft," "rough," "smooth," and "bumpy" to describe the textures of the different surfaces. The sensor (or sensors) stimulated by each texture sends a message to a particular part of his brain, which makes him feel each specific sensation.

YOU WILL NEED: **1**
- blindfold
- touch strip
- assistant

YOU WILL NEED: golf ball,
- blindfold   ping-pong
- gloves   ball, tomato,
- objects of   small apple,
  similar   racquetball
  shape, e.g.,   - assistant

2

IDENTIFYING BY FEEL

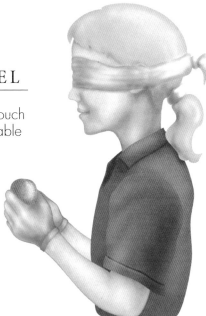

How easy is it to identify objects by touch alone, without the benefit of being able to see? Here's your chance to find out.

1 Blindfold your assistant.

2 Hand him each object in turn. Ask him to feel each one carefully and attempt to identify it. Can he?

3 Repeat the experiment, this time with your assistant wearing gloves.

WHAT HAPPENS?

Without being able to see, your assistant should find identification more difficult. Differences in texture, however, can help him, for example, the dimpled surface of the golf ball. Hardness, such as the fleshy feel of a tomato, is another useful guide. Gloves make identification more difficult because they "blur" the textures.

3

TWO-POINT TEST

Are all parts of the body equally sensitive to touch? Find out using the two-point test.

1 Unfold a paper clip as shown to produce two points about a quarter-inch apart.

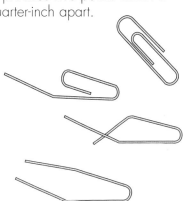

2 Blindfold your assistant. Gently touch different parts of his skin and ask him how many points he can feel in each place.

WHAT HAPPENS?

In some parts of the body, such as the fingertips, he will feel two distinct points, whereas in others, such as the back, he will feel only one. This is because touch receptors are not evenly distributed. The fingertips have many more than the back, so the fingers can clearly distinguish between the two points.

TOUCH

Without its skeleton, your body would collapse into a shapeless blob! Learn about the bony framework that supports you, lets you move, and protects your internal organs.

DYNAMIC SKELETON

About 206 bones make up your skeleton. Most meet at flexible joints that allow them to move when they are pulled by muscles. Bones are not dry and dusty. They are moist, living organs that have a structure—solid on the outside but honeycombed on the inside—that makes them both light and strong.

Hollow core filled with bone marrow

Light but strong, spongy bone on the inside

Hard, compact bone on the outside

Cross section of a bone

1

HARD OR FLEXIBLE?

Each bone has two main components that work together to make it both hard and flexible. Try this experiment to separate the two parts.

1 Ask an adult to clean a thin chicken bone. Try bending the bone. What happens?

2 Using cotton thread and a pencil, suspend the bone inside a jar. Fill the jar with vinegar. Leave the jar for 24 hours.

3 Remove the bone from the vinegar and wash it. Try to bend it. What do you notice?

WHAT HAPPENS?

The bone is more flexible than before. The overnight soaking in vinegar—a weak acid—removed the calcium salts that make the bone hard. This leaves behind collagen, a material that is tough but flexible.

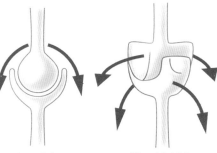

2
EXPLORING JOINTS

Joints enable you to move. But do some joints allow more movement than others?

1 Carefully move your assistant's lower leg to see the range of movement the knee joint allows.

2 Repeat this with your assistant's arm at the shoulder, and with his thumb where it meets the palm.

Hinge joint   **Ellipsoidal joint**

WHAT HAPPENS?
The knee joint (a hinge joint) only allows forward and backward bending movements. The shoulder joint is the most flexible in the body and is a ball-and-socket joint that allows virtually unlimited movement. The thumb joint is an ellipsoidal joint and allows movement backward and forward and from side to side.

3
LOCKED TOGETHER

Not all joints in the body can be moved. Use the jigsaw puzzle pieces to mimic the bones that make up the skull.

1 Take two pieces of the jigsaw puzzle and fit them together on a flat surface.

2 Hold each piece with one hand and try to move the pieces against each other.

Suture between skull bones

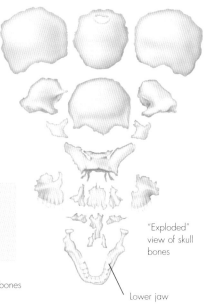

"Exploded" view of skull bones

Lower jaw

WHAT HAPPENS?
There is little movement because the curved edges of the jigsaw pieces fit together tightly. All but one of the 22 bones in your skull are locked together by jigsaw-like joints, called sutures, *to make the skull. The skull surrounds your brain and forms your face's strong framework. The other bone in your skull is the freely moving lower jaw.*

FRAMEWORK

BONY

LABORATORY

9

All your body's movements, from blinking an eye to running with a football, are produced by muscles. Muscles are unique because they can contract (get shorter) and pull.

MOVERS AND SUPPORTERS

More than 650 muscles are attached to the bones of your skeleton by tough tendons. When they contract—under instructions from your brain—they pull across joints and your body moves. Some muscles also support your body and keep it upright.

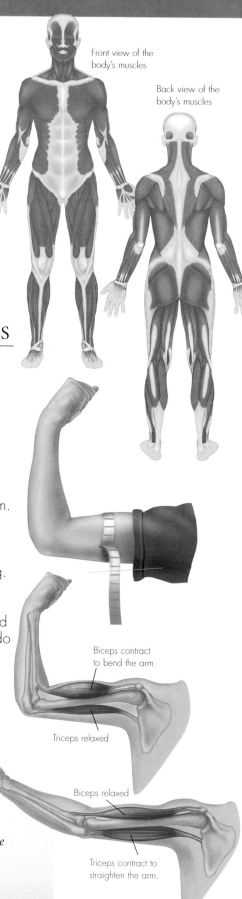

Front view of the body's muscles

Back view of the body's muscles

OPPOSING MUSCLES

Muscles can only pull, not push. They work in pairs, each with an action opposite to the other.

1 Put your hand over the front of your assistant's upper arm and squeeze gently.

2 Ask your assistant to bend his arm. What do you feel?

3 Measure the distance around the upper arm before and after bending.

4 Hold the back of his upper arm and squeeze gently. Ask him to bend and then straighten his arm. What do you feel?

Biceps contract to bend the arm.

Triceps relaxed

Biceps relaxed

Triceps contract to straighten the arm.

WHAT HAPPENS?
When the arm bends, you can feel the biceps muscles at the front of the upper arm getting shorter and fatter as they pull on the bones of the forearm. When the arm straightens, you can feel the opposite muscles in the pair, the triceps, pulling the forearm downward.

YOU WILL NEED: ①
• tape measure
• assistant

YOU WILL NEED: ②
• bathroom scale
• assistant

YOU WILL NEED: ③
• assistant

② WHICH IS STRONGEST?

Your body's muscles vary enormously in size and strength. Try comparing the strength of different sets of muscles.

1 Press the scale as hard as you can, using the palms of your hands. Ask your assistant to note the reading.

2 Repeat this process using other parts of the body, e.g., between the knees or pushing with your feet against a wall.

WHAT HAPPENS?

The scale measures the strength of your muscles. You should find, for example, that the muscles that pull your legs inward are weakest, and your thigh muscles are strongest. The harder the job, the stronger the muscles.

③ KNEE JERK

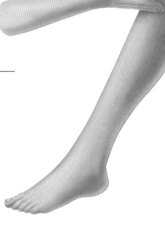

Reflex actions are fast, unchanging, and automatic (see pages 6–7). Here's a reflex that is used in walking.

1 Ask your assistant to sit down and cross one leg over the other.

2 With the edge of your open hand, gently tap his knee on the spot just below the kneecap. Do you notice anything?

WHAT HAPPENS?

If you tap in the right place, your assistant's lower leg should jerk upward. When you tap his knee, you stretch a tendon. This sends a message to his brain, which sends an instruction to his thigh muscles to contract and make the lower leg move. This happens automatically every time you walk.

POWER

MUSCLE

LABORATORY 10

Your body has its own internal transport network, the circulatory system. As you will see, it delivers a nonstop supply of food and oxygen to every one of your body cells. It also helps defend your body from germs.

CIRCULATORY SYSTEM

Your muscular heart pumps blood around a network of living tubes called *blood vessels*. Arteries carry blood away from the heart, while veins bring it back. The two are linked by tiny capillaries. Blood consists of liquid plasma, which carries food; red blood cells, which carry oxygen; and white blood cells, which fight infection.

Plasma

White blood cells

Red blood cells

Blood vessel

DID YOU KNOW?

One drop of blood contains 250 million red blood cells. Red blood cells are produced by your bones at the rate of 2 million per second.

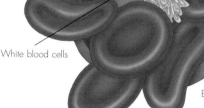

1

PULSE RATE

Here's a quick way of counting the number of times your heart beats every minute.

1 Sit down. Put two fingers on the underside of your wrist, just below your thumb.

2 Feel carefully until you detect a regular beat or pulse.

3 Count the number of beats in 15 seconds. Multiply this by 4 to find the number of beats per minute.

WHAT HAPPENS?

You were pressing on an artery where it passes just under the skin and over a bone. Every time your heart beat, you felt blood being pushed along the artery. This is known as a pulse. You should have counted between 50 and 80 pulsations— and heartbeats—per minute.

TRY THIS

Run on the spot for 2 minutes and repeat the steps above. Your heart rate increases. When you exercise, your muscles work harder and need extra fuel and oxygen. To provide this, your heart beats faster.

22

2

TOUGH MUSCLE

Your heart beats for a whole lifetime without stopping to rest. See whether the muscles that move your fingers could do the same thing.

1 Clench your fingers into a fist and then open them.

2 Repeat this as quickly as you can, for as long as you can. What do you notice?

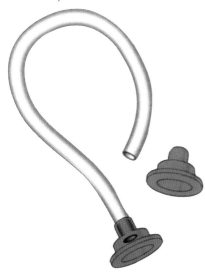

WHAT HAPPENS?
You should hear the sound of your assistant's heart beating. Each heartbeat produces two sounds, a longer "lubb" sound and a shorter "dupp" sound. These sounds are made when the heart's valves close to keep the blood from flowing backward.

WHAT HAPPENS?
The skeletal muscles that move your fingers soon tire and you have to stop. But your heart is powered by cardiac muscle, which contracts without tiring.

DID YOU KNOW?
If they could be stretched out, your blood vessels would go around the earth two and a half times!

3

HEART BEAT

Doctors listen to the heart beating to see if it is working properly. You can do the same here.

1 Put the earpieces of the stethoscope in your ears.

2 Put the other end firmly against your assistant's chest. Can you hear anything?

BLOOD

LIFE

Every second of every day, a process called *cell respiration* is happening inside your cells. It "burns up" glucose to release the energy that cells need to work. To do this, the cells need one vital ingredient—oxygen.

Throat

Trachea (windpipe)

Lung

MOVING AIR

Getting oxygen into the body is the job of your respiratory system. It carries air into your lungs. Here oxygen passes into your blood to be carried to your cells, and carbon dioxide—the waste product of cell respiration—passes out of it. Air is moved in and out of your lungs by breathing.

1
STEAMY BREATH

The air you breathe out contains more carbon dioxide (and less oxygen) than the air you breathe in. What else is different about it?

1 Take the mirror and hold it about 3 inches away from your face.

2 Breathe out through your mouth onto the mirror. What do you see?

WHAT HAPPENS?
The mirror starts to become cloudy. This is because water vapor, picked up from the moist lining of the tubes inside your lungs, has condensed as a mist of water droplets on the cool mirror.

YOU WILL NEED: **1**
• mirror

YOU WILL NEED: **2**
• tape measure
• assistant

YOU WILL NEED: **3**
• stopwatch or
  watch showing
  seconds

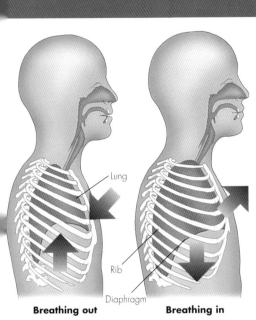

Lung

Rib

Diaphragm

Breathing out   **Breathing in**

WHAT HAPPENS?

*As he breathes in, your
assistant's chest gets
bigger. Muscles between
the ribs pull them upward and
outward (and the muscular, dome-
shaped diaphragm gets flatter),
making the space inside the chest
and lungs bigger, so he sucks in air
from the outside.*

2

EXPANDING CHEST

What happens to the chest
when you breathe in and
out? It's time to find out!

1 Put a tape measure around
you assistant's chest at its
widest part.

2 Ask your assistant to breathe
out as much as possible. Take
a chest measurement.

3 Ask him to take a deep
breath. Take another chest
measurement.

3

OUT OF BREATH

You breathe in and out
automatically without
noticing that you are doing it.
Does your breathing rate always
stay the same?

1 Using the stopwatch, count
the number of times you breathe
in one minute.

2 Run in place for 3 minutes.
During the last minute, count the
number of breaths you take. Has
your breathing rate changed?

WHAT HAPPENS?
*When resting you
probably breathe
between 12 and 18 times a
minute. During exercise your
breathing rate increases so that
you get more oxygen into your
lungs and bloodstream. Extra
oxygen is needed by your
muscles to release the energy
required to make you run.*

BREATHS

DEEP

LABORATORY 12

You need to eat in order to live. Food provides your body with energy and the ability to grow, repair itself, and keep warm. But eating is just the first part of the process.

DIGESTIVE SYSTEM

Your digestive system processes food so that it can be used by your body. Food is chewed in your mouth and churned up in your stomach to produce a soupy liquid that is digested. Digestion breaks food down into simple molecules as it is squeezed along your small intestine. These molecules are absorbed into your bloodstream, which delivers them to your ever-hungry cells.

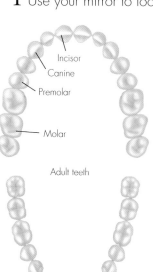

Ball of food pushed by muscles from throat to stomach

Esophagus

Esophagus

Stomach

Small intestine

1

HOW MANY TEETH?

Imagine how difficult it would be to eat without teeth! But are all teeth the same? Have a look and find out.

1 Use your mirror to look inside your mouth.

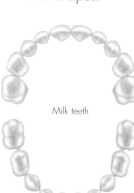

Incisor

Canine

Premolar

Molar

Adult teeth

Milk teeth

2 Count your teeth—both the upper and lower sets—and look at their shapes.

WHAT HAPPENS?
Everyone has two sets of teeth in their lifetime, milk teeth and then adult teeth. Both sets contain different types of teeth. Thin incisors cut food, canines grip it, and premolars and molars crush and grind it.

YOU WILL NEED: **1**
• mirror

YOU WILL NEED: **2**
• slice of white bread

YOU WILL NEED: **3**
• temperature strip
• assistant

2
CHEMICAL BREAKDOWN

Apart from the action of the teeth and the churning of stomach walls, another process is at work to break down food into simple molecules. What is it?

1 Put a piece of white bread in your mouth. Note its taste.

2 Chew the bread for two minutes without swallowing. What does it taste like now?

WHAT HAPPENS?
At first the starchy bread tastes bland. But after a couple of minutes it will taste sweeter. This is because an enzyme (a chemical digester) in your saliva (spit) breaks down starch in the bread into simpler, sweet sugars. Other enzymes are also at work in your stomach and small intestine.

3
HEAT PRODUCTION

Food provides cells with the chemical energy they need to work. But is that the only type of energy that's involved?

1 Put the temperature strip on your assistant's forehead.

2 Make a note of the final temperature reading when you can see no further change to the strip.

WHAT HAPPENS?
The temperature strip should give a reading of about 98.6°F. This is the normal temperature inside the human body. Some of the energy released in cells from food is heat energy, and it's this that keeps the body warm regardless of the temperature outside.

TRY THIS
Try putting the temperature strip on different parts of your body, e.g., your foot, stomach, or armpit. Do you notice a change in the temperature at certain places?

PROCESSING

FOOD

When human beings reproduce, they pass on their individual characteristics to their children. The attributes of both parents play a role in the development of each new offspring.

FAMILY CONNECTIONS

Ever noticed the likenesses within families? That's because parents pass on certain characteristics to their children. They do this through their chromosomes.

Chromosomes are packages of instructions, called *genes*, that are found inside every body cell. Genes control your hair and skin color, as well as thousands of other characteristics.

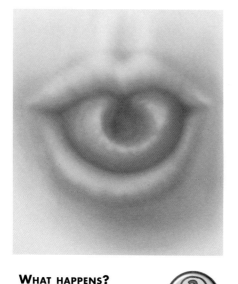

WHAT HAPPENS?
You will find that people can either roll their tongue or not. There is no in-between stage. If you can roll your tongue, you may find that most of your family members can roll theirs, as well, because this is an inherited characteristic.

1

TONGUE ROLLERS

Many body characteristics, such as skin color, show a wide range of variation because each is controlled by a number of genes. Others are very clear-cut because they are controlled by a single pair of genes. Here's one to investigate:

1 Look into the mirror and stick out your tongue. See if you can roll your tongue lengthways into a *U*-shape.

2 See if your friends and family can roll their tongues.

DID YOU KNOW?
You share 99.9% of your genes with other humans, 98% with chimpanzees, 90% with mice and rats, 85% with zebra fish, 36% with fruit flies, and 7% with E. coli, a tiny bacterium. As you can see, all living things have something in common.

Whorl

Loop

Arch

Composite (mixture)

YOU WILL NEED: ①
- family and friends

YOU WILL NEED: ②
- ink pad
- paper
- magnifying glass

YOU WILL NEED: ③
- colored beads
- two bowls or other containers
- blindfold

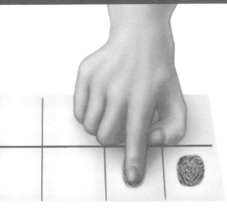

③ GIRL OR BOY?

Every body cell contains 23 pairs of chromosomes. One pair consists of the sex chromosomes, called X and Y, that determine whether you are a girl or boy. See how this happens.

1 Put ten red beads in one bowl, and five red beads and five blue beads in the other.

2 Put on the blindfold. Carefully pick out one bead from each bowl and put the pair on the table.

3 Repeat until the containers are empty.

② FINGERPRINTS

Fingerprints are patterns produced by curved lines of sweat left behind by the ridges on your fingertips. Are everyone's fingerprints the same?

1 Roll your right thumb on the ink pad, then roll it on a piece of paper to produce a fingerprint.

2 Repeat this with your other fingers and thumb in order. Label each print.

3 Repeat Steps 1 and 2 with your friends and family.

4 Look at the fingerprints with the magnifying glass.

WHAT HAPPENS?
Your inky fingerprints will show patterns of whorls, loops, and arches (see picture). None of your fingerprints will be the same, nor will they match those of your friends or family (even if you have an identical twin with whom you share the same genes). The shapes of fingertip ridges are determined not by your genes but by the conditions inside your mother's uterus (womb). That's why everyone has different fingerprints.

WHAT HAPPENS?
You will have five blue/red pairs and five red/red pairs. Each bead represents a sex chromosome: red = X, and blue = Y. A female has XX chromosomes and a male has XY chromosomes. Each container represented a parent (blue/red = father, red/red = mother). That means that parents have an equal chance of having either a girl or a boy.

GENERATIONS

NEW

Modern medicine uses all sorts of techniques to help treat disease. Here you can learn about some of the modern methods doctors use, and also what the future might hold for the human body.

SEEING INSIDE

There was a time when doctors would have to cut open a body to see what was happening inside it. Then in 1895 a German scientist discovered X rays, which enabled doctors to "see" bones inside a living body. Today there are several different imaging techniques that allow doctors to see not just bones but other living tissues. The patient below is inside a CT scanner, which produces an image of a "slice" of the body.

CT scanning machine

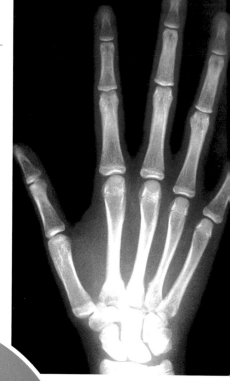

X ray of a hand

REPLACEMENT PARTS

If a body part is faulty or damaged, it is becoming easier for doctors to replace it. Made using modern materials, these replacement parts include false teeth, false joints, and artificial limbs. A person can have a "robotic" or artificial arm that responds to signals from their nerves and muscles, which make the artificial fingers move.

2
INSTRUCTION PACK

Inside every body cell is a set of instructions for making and operating a human body, called the *genome*. Each instruction—and there are thousands of them—is contained in a single gene. Recently, scientists have been working on the Human Genome Project and have started to find out what each gene does, and to reveal the tiny differences in the genome from person to person. In the future each of us can know the details of our own genetic makeup.

One of the many strands of DNA molecules found inside each body cell

3
MINIATURE EXPLORERS

Tiny "nanorobots" may have a role to play in the medicine of the future. Acting like a miniature submarine, the nanorobot would travel along a person's blood vessels. If it found any damage to the blood vessel, such as a blockage, it would send a message to the doctor and then fix the problem.

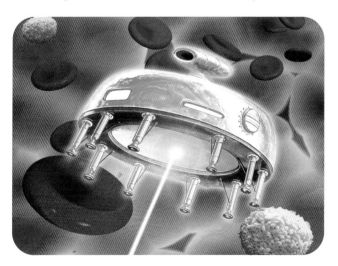

Artist's impression of a nanorobot unblocking a blood vessel

BODIES

- **Blind spot** Part of the retina where the optic nerve leaves the eye and there are no light sensors.
- **Brain** Part of the nervous system that receives and processes information from sensors, and sends out instructions to control body activities.
- **Calcium** Mineral that forms the hard part of bones and teeth.
- **Carbon dioxide** Waste product of cell respiration that is breathed out from the lungs.
- **Cell** Tiny living units, trillions of which make up a human body.
- **Cell respiration** A process that releases energy inside cells from glucose and other foods using oxygen.
- **Chromosome** One of 46 threadlike structures found inside every body cell that contains the instructions to build and run the body.
- **Collagen** Tough, fibrous protein found in tendons, bone, and skin.
- **Cone** Light sensor found in the retina of the eye that provides color vision.
- **CT (computerized tomography) scan** Special type of X ray that produces images of slices of living tissues.
- **Dermis** Thicker, lower layer of the skin that contains sensors.
- **Diaphragm** Sheet of muscle that separates the chest from the abdomen and plays a part in breathing.
- **Energy** The ability to cause an action, needed by the body to make it work.
- **Enzyme** Chemical that speeds up the breakdown of food during digestion.
- **Epidermis** Thinner, upper layer of the skin.
- **Gene** One of 50,000 instructions, found in the chromosomes, for building and running the body.
- **Genome** Complete set of genes found in the body.
- **Joint** Part of the skeleton where one or more bones meet.
- **Molecule** Tiny chemical particle made up of two or more linked atoms.
- **Neuron** One of billions of linked nerve cells that form the nervous system.
- **Organ** Body part, such as stomach or heart, made up of different tissues.
- **Oxygen** Gas taken from breathed-in air and used during cell respiration.
- **Reflex action** Rapid, automatic action, such as blinking, that often protects the body from harm.
- **Rod** Light sensor found in the retina of the eye, which provides black-and-white vision.
- **Skeletal muscle** Type of muscle that moves the bones of the skeleton.
- **Sound wave** Vibration that passes through the air and is detected by the ears.
- **Stethoscope** Instrument used to listen to heartbeats and breathing.
- **System** Linked organs that work together to carry out certain tasks.
- **Tissue** Group of one type of cell that works together to perform a particular task.
- **X ray** Type of radiation that reveals bones inside the living body.